More Than a Million
Grace Farris

BLOOMSBURY
CHILDREN'S BOOKS
NEW YORK LONDON OXFORD NEW DELHI SYDNEY

BLOOMSBURY CHILDREN'S BOOKS
Bloomsbury Publishing Inc., part of Bloomsbury Publishing Plc
1359 Broadway, New York, NY 10018
50 Bedford Square, London, WC1B 3DP, UK
Bloomsbury Publishing Ireland Limited, 29 Earlsfort Terrace, Dublin 2, D02 AY28, Ireland

BLOOMSBURY, BLOOMSBURY CHILDREN'S BOOKS, and the Diana logo
are trademarks of Bloomsbury Publishing Plc

First published in the United States of America in January 2026
by Bloomsbury Children's Books

Text and illustrations copyright © 2026 by Grace Farris

All rights reserved. No part of this publication may be: i) reproduced or transmitted in any form, electronic or mechanical, including photocopying, recording, or by means of any information storage or retrieval system without prior permission in writing from the publishers; or ii) used or reproduced in any way for the training, development, or operation of artificial intelligence (AI) technologies, including generative AI technologies. The rights holders expressly reserve this publication from the text and data mining exception as per Article 4(3) of the Digital Single Market Directive (EU) 2019/790.

Bloomsbury books may be purchased for business or promotional use. For information on bulk purchases please contact Macmillan Corporate and Premium Sales Department at specialmarkets@macmillan.com

Library of Congress Cataloging-in-Publication Data available upon request
ISBN 978-1-5476-1791-3 (hardcover) • ISBN 978-1-5476-1792-0 (e-book)
ISBN 978-1-5476-1793-7 (e-pdf)

Art created digitally with an Apple Pencil using Autodesk Sketchbook
Typeset in a font created by Grace Farris based on her handwriting
Book design by John Candell
Printed in China by Leo Paper Products, Heshan, Guangdong
10 9 8 7 6 5 4 3 2 1

To find out more about our authors and books visit www.bloomsbury.com and sign up for our newsletters. For product safety-related questions contact productsafety@bloomsbury.com.

Mommm. I had a bad dream. I dreamed you didn't love me.

Love you more than a hundred "good nights," "sweet dreams," "farewells," "adieus"

Love you more than a million "I love yous."

Love you more than a boatload of books about llamas

Love you more than a million bubbles in the bath

Love you more than a thousand carefully made grilled cheeses

Love you more than approximately twenty-four hundred dinosaur names

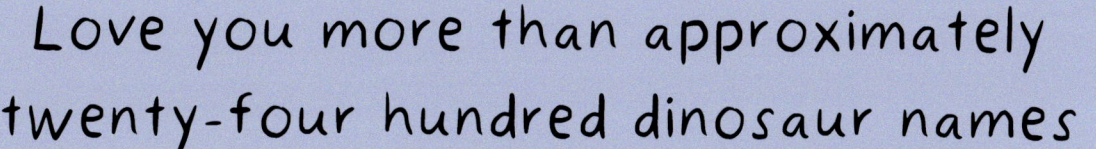

Love you more than a bunch of . . .

Love you more than the countless leaky sippy cups

Love you more than just one more
goodbye at the school door

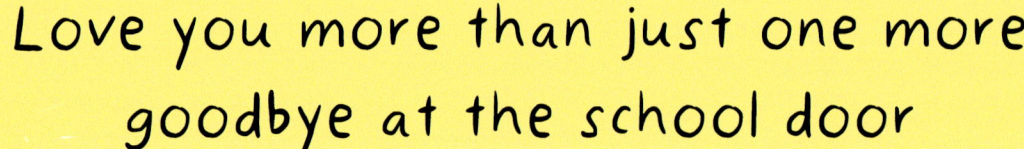

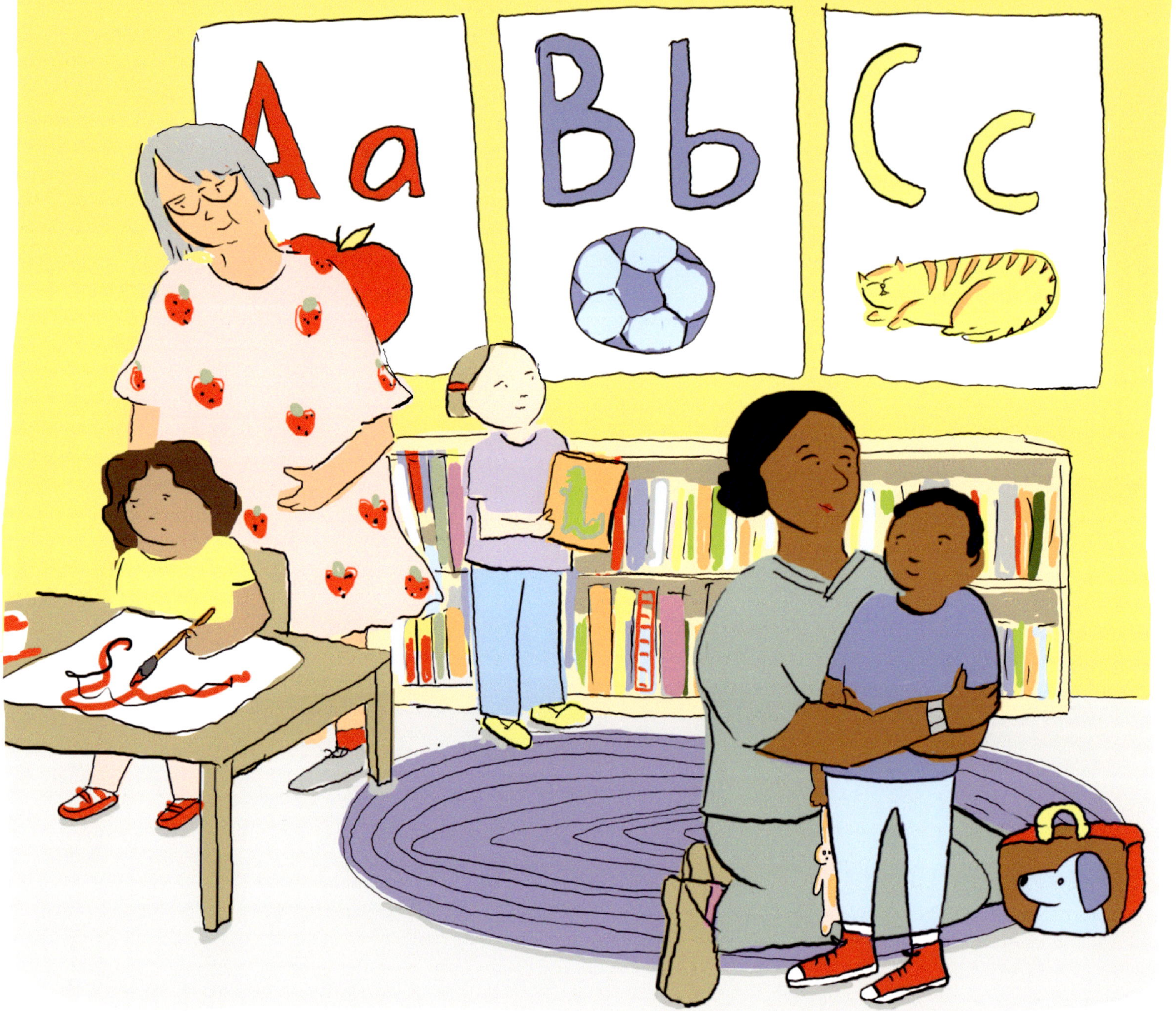

Love you more than one . . . two . . .
three more five-minute warnings

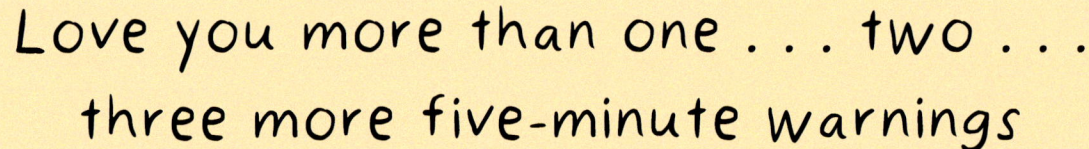

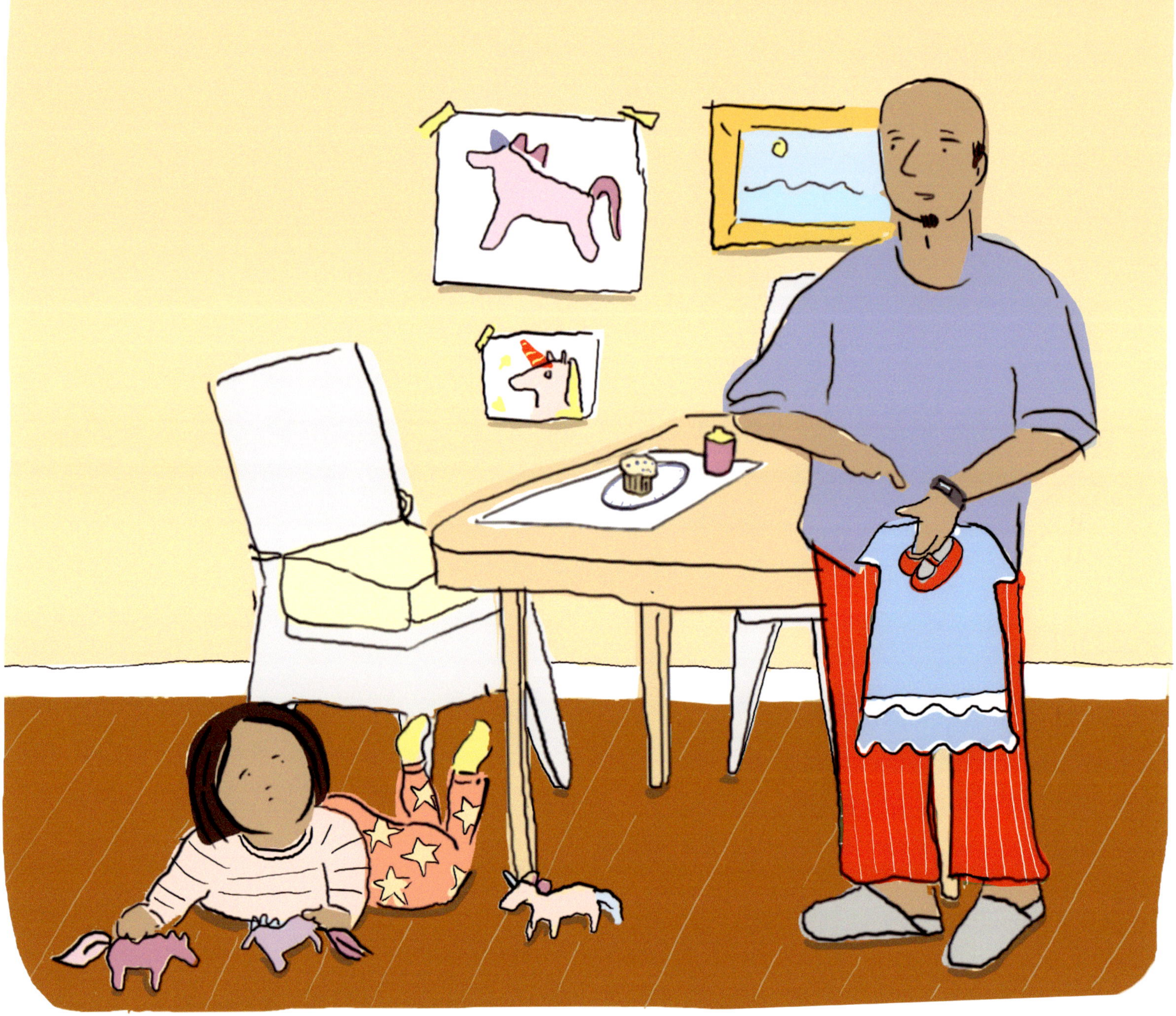

Love you more than a million very early mornings

for George and Russ